THE SECRET RED RAIDER

RICHARD A. BOEHLER, JR.

authorHOUSE®

AuthorHouse™
1663 Liberty Drive
Bloomington, IN 47403
www.authorhouse.com
Phone: 833-262-8899

Published by AuthorHouse   09/08/2022

ISBN: 978-1-6655-7018-3 (sc)
ISBN: 978-1-6655-7017-6 (e)

Print information available on the last page.

Any people depicted in stock imagery provided by Getty Images are models, and such images are being used for illustrative purposes only.
Certain stock imagery © Getty Images.

This book is printed on acid-free paper.

Contents

Acknowledgements

1. **The music.** To all the band directors, at all levels of education = for leadership, guidance and experience in the "wind ensembles". Concerts were amazing and marching bands were a challenge (e.g., choreography during marching band competitions). The band members always worked hard to learn the music. The friendships and love are forever embedded in memories.

2. **The football team and weight room.** To all the coaches, at all levels of sports = for leadership, guidance and the experience of "discipline" and "teamwork". Every sore ankle, broken bone, dislocated shoulder, bump and bruise was worth it.

3. **The United States Military.** For the topnotch, unique training of this great nation: The United States of America. All heart and soul. "Honor, Courage and Commitment". Need I say more?

4. **To the University.** For the breadth of knowledge and depth of wisdom shared through various academic curriculum. The challenges were many and the experiences gained offered a path to "higher level thinking", which is essential in this world. To the dedicated professors, assistants and all levels of staff: the diligent efforts really made a difference in many students lives. Late night labs to learn the blood flow through chambers of the human heart, dissections of dog sharks, titrations with chemicals and a variety of unique laboratory techniques taught students the "way of science" (i.e., the scientific method). And all this is carried with each student throughout life.

5. **To all the great writers.** I always enjoyed Michael Crichton and Stephenie Meyer. Especially, Stephen King (S.K.). For leadership and the many samples of what it means to be a good writer. Specifically, the guidance of S.K. impacted me in the following way: (paraphrasing) = write a lot and read a lot. Write, even if it amounts to nothing more than a pile of **IT. Keep writing. And that inspired me to at least give it a go, utilize what I know and reach deep inside to be creative. My whole life has admired such creative leaders. The creativity is wonderful in this life, and it is also seen in great art, heard in innovative music, displayed in unique characters of movies and created within innovative science.

6. **Wisdom.** For teaching a wild child the true meaning of being humble. In teaching that a rough boy could in

fact grow to be a person "they never thought he could be" = "a gentleman" (Although, always part wolf).

7. To the mystery of "Faith".

A Reunion

It was a dark, cool night as he pulled into the parking lot. He hadn't seen Gina in six months. She had called to ask him to meet her at the funeral home in Patchogue, New York. When he took the call, he was in little creek Virginia. The storm had finally passed. The waters off the coast, in the Atlantic-ocean were something fierce. Even the largest United States Navy ships would struggle to stay afloat in such rough waters. The oiler was the "USS Monongahela", a monster of a ship. A large ship that transported oil and supplies to sister ships [horizontal supplies replenishment]. If placed next to a commercial cruise ship [like the carnival cruise line], she would tower over her by two to four times in size.

The ship was attempting to avoid the hurricane... mother nature had other plans for her. The waters were incredibly rough. The seas were reaching such great heights. These types of ocean waves, with extreme crests were the types found near distant island shores [during violent storms]. The ship was somewhere in the Atlantic and it "rocked", it "rolled", relentlessly – forever [it seemed]. With experience, good skill and determination – the ship made her way back to the calm shores of Virginia, as the storm eventually passed. Tommy left the ship with his buddies. They did not have legs. They attempted to regain their legs, as they walked around Virginia Beach [the sea took their legs. They called it: sea legs]. The local Virginia towns were completely flooded with sea water. Many stores were closed. One of Tommy's friends, was active-duty military. A guy from the west coast, California. A good group of guys that were proud to serve the great country, USA. A good group of guys that also liked to have some fun.

The active-duty buddies were renting an apartment, not too far from the Navy Base. They walked around the town, bought plenty of beer for the night festivities. Tommy and his buddy were looking to get a fresh tattoo. They settled on an ear piercing instead. At the Virginia Beach apartment - they chugged beer in large tubes, attached to funnels.

That was when Tommy received the call from Gina. She was upset. One of her closest friends had suddenly died. She asked Tommy to meet her at the funeral home.He soothed her with brief conversation: "of course, I will be there within a day". The funeral viewing was planned for five days from the telephone call. Tommy softly wished her a peaceful night, with a hug [spoken through the phone, but certainly felt over the distance in space/time]. He did not feel like chugging any more beer after the telephone call. The conversation was brief, but rattled him. What had happened now in that God forsaken place? It had been six months since Gina broke up with Tommy. For him, it was like one day had passed – not six months. They did not say much on the telephone... it was a good silence that amazingly reconnected them [he thought, if that was even possible].

Tommy watched the television in his friend's apartment, late into the evening. He could not get something out of his mind. While he was out in the rough seas, rocking and rolling – he was listening to early 50s rock music. He loved the saxophone solos from the 1950s+. There was a Beetles song... "do you want to know a secret", then another "birthday song... Happy, Happy birthday baby..." that played. He thought it was probably just a coincidence. Or, maybe not a coincidence. The songs seemed to somehow bridge a place in time between two people. A "preparation" of events that would happen... and a day or so after the songs were played, Tommy received the call from Gina. Are there coincidences in life? Yes and No. People cross paths in life for a reason or for many reasons? The Beetles song was one of "their songs..." and the "Birthday song" was the song played... the last time they loved each other [her last birthday gift – the last time their souls connected during the gentle passionate love they shared]. He fell asleep. Tommy and his sailor buddies had to report to the ship for inspection at 0715 – in fresh ironed uniforms.

The trip back to Long Island was fast. Tommy caught a military flight up the coast in the middle of the night. His training for that mission was complete. He helped, he learned, he performed... it was over – for now.

As a reservist, the orders were not "every week". It was "once a month". The missions were sometimes local [in the NY area], and other times... the missions were global [everywhere, anywhere on the planet...].

She was standing there, right outside the funeral home. Her dress was really a short tight black skirt. Her eyes were wet with fresh tears as she entered Tommy's car. They sat in the car for some time. She immediately fell into his arms, with hugs and passionate kisses...

A large crowd of people were arriving in waves, parking their cars and entering the funeral home. It was the community. The crowd consisted of family, of friends, of students, coaches, teachers and many others. It just didn't seem right, for such a young guy to die. Tommy and Gina remained in the car as the sky opened – and the thunder rolled. It was an odd roll of thunder. Tommy had visited many places around the globe and experienced various storms. These clouds were different…very grey.

Although, it was evening – and the darkness may have shadowed the clouds that way… The rain was coming down in buckets, as the lightning flashed in the skies above. Tommy had a seventh sense for certain things. This was one of those things. Something was not right. He did not present his feelings to Gina. Rather, he listened more to her – as she talked. She spoke of a time they met in another state. "Remember touring the windy city, in a fancy limo?" He smiled, "of course!

That's all you remember?" She laughed, "no, it's just that the rain in the Chicago area fell this way…, it reminded me o – she stopped as an incredible bolt of lightning traveled through the sky to hit a nearby tree!". She pressed her body into his, as the storm continued to thrive outside the car. Her body was shaking when she cuddled into Tommy. Shortly after the embrace, a stillness and warmth ensued... She was comfortable, calm and content – for that moment [anyway, Tommy wanted to believe that].

You know, come to think of it – I do remember that the Garth Brooks song "The Thunder Rolls" was playing in the limo! Tommy asked Gina if she remembered. Her voice was muffled, being pressed deep in his torso. Tommy heard her muffle though – "Of Course, DORK!" Tommy smiled and could see her soft, inviting brown eyes in his visions [even though her eyes were hidden]. Tommy continued, thinking that the conversation was calming the terrible circumstances that surrounded them... I never wanted to rent that limo! That's not me. It was my friend, Kenny. A good guy, with expensive tastes. Maybe not... "I don't know... I think he just wanted to enjoy a day in Chicago; especially after three grueling months of intense training – with isolation". The limo was nice, I mean – you know, the music, the company – the company... She giggled, and replied "why are you repeating yourself?"

Must be a subconscious thing... just want to make the point that I always enjoyed the company of a pretty brown eyed girl! They laughed and hugged even closer, even deeper.

They decided to go into the funeral home. It was tough to get out of the car and enter the place. Inside the home there was little room to even find an empty seat. They paid their respects to the family, to her friend. Tommy knew her friend – but not that well. He thought that she was taking this really hard. Tommy sensed that there was more to the circumstances. It was not just a seventh sense, not just a feeling. He could see the way Gina tensed up when surrounded by the community. She seemed "frightened". Gina and Tommy didn't really stay too long, at her request.

In Tommy's car Gina asked if he could meet at her house – she wanted to drive her car home, then head out to the north shore beach. She kissed him deeply, passionately on his lips! Just like that, six months turned to zero months – they were together (Tommy thought that maybe they were back together, weren't they?). The thunder rolled further away, in the distance. The storm had passed and the environment quickly changed to cool – refreshing breezes. Gina changed her clothes, sporting a school spirited sweatshirt with blue jeans. She brought an extra sweatshirt for Tommy. They left her parent's house and drove to the north shore beach of Long Island, together...

The drive to the north shore was short, taking only about twenty minutes. The roads were empty and the sky was dark with storm clouds. Tommy and Gina had travelled the "main 112 road" many nights before.

It was a nice road, a silent road. Not too many stores along side the road as they drove. Once in a while, the road did have its hazards. Tommy drove north and south, during early mornings and late nights... On occasion, in the late evening [after 10 PM], wild animals tended to cross in areas of the black top... quick rabbits tried their luck by playing chicken with traffic (which consisted of one or two cars, at most). Larger animals that impacted a car in the eve would cause a crash with total car destruction... There used to be many more farms in the northern section of this mid island area (that is – half way through the island, at the start of SUFFOLK COUNTY) – where apple picking and strawberry gathering sparked the interests of visitors... Some of the local farms remained, others did not. Tourists and locals could travel further east on the island to enjoy the more robust farms.

Just prior to entering the furthest northern point on 112, was a local coffee shop. It was situated not far from a bowling alley. Gina and Tommy enjoyed midnight bowling on Friday nights. Many high school students had enjoyed the entertainment (it was a necessity, to keep the sanity of the teenager – and the sanity of pretty much all ages...). Where else could you listen to a variety of music in the dark, under strobe lights...bowl a few games, and get a buzz with the facilities dark beer...

Tommy parked the car outside the local Port Jeff coffee shop (the long island 7-11). Gina waited in the car as Tommy ran in to get two hot coffees. He hugged her passionately, prior to leaving the car – the warmth was returned one hundred-fold [and was felt 1000 times, straight to his heart and soul]. As he approached the front door of the coffee shop he smiled. He had just visited a similar coffee shop in Virginia, before boarding the US Navy

Ship. The coffee shop down in Virginia was similar in many ways...except the big sign on the front of the store was the local "WAWA". It was the simple things, like coffee shop names, that gave him a chuckle – which lightened his inner light, his inner soul...

Not to far from the 7-11, they arrived at their final destination. The beach was dark and silent, with the exception of small crashing ocean waves. They placed the blanket on the sand – close to the water and sipped their vanilla flavored coffee. The coffee matched Gina's sweet-scented vanilla perfume. Tommy got right into the conversation, with sad looking eyes... "what happened in this fucking place... this time?" Gina innately reacted with an uncomfortable smirk. But, quickly changed her expression – realizing who was talking to her. She knew Tommy... She knew him well. And she started the conversation with just that, what she was thinking. She would not talk of local happenings, with anyone – unless it was someone she could trust. Tommy smiled and then gently grabbed her hand. He said: "how's the coffee?" She replied: "How can you do that?" It was his way to lighten the thick atmosphere, the area of surrounding darkness… He continued [hoping it would help her reach a calm, comfortable feeling]. The truth, you want the truth – I know, and it is really simple for me…Tommy built on his initial sting of words to her. Simply… you know me, you knew me before I was scorched! There are things that you would not believe! There are things in this world that would make you cringe with uneasiness… And I bear that. However, knowing that the light connection of a time of innocence exists… helps calm my soul, helps relieve some of the burden. There are many things to be grateful for, so don't get me wrong… It's just that, sometimes… it's the thought of returning to a simpler place in time that puts a smile on my face. A time where I wake early on a Saturday morning, pump iron in the gym, pop amino acids, shower...then drive to your house...climb a story outside the house and knock on your window. She stopped him. We know what happens after that! They both smiled and agreed that was something to be happy about.

So, she chimed in with the town dirt. Another accident, another death. A suspicious death with odd circumstances. And what's even more odd. She started noticing that in the late evenings...she stopped. It's as though she was incredibly frightened to continue her conversation. But, she did continue... It was as if the dead returned! She didn't know that this was a fact. It was more of an intuition, more of a theory and a suspicion – based on some frightening happenings in the local Suffolk County towns. Gina had remembered a study she read, where if you looked around the globe, you could find a similar person. The similarity was not of the soul, not of the mind and heart. It was just a "stunt double". A person that just had a few basic visual traits... Tommy laughed because he had the "familiar face".

People often stopped him to find out that he was not the person they Had been looking for. It was just a similar style, a similar look... or maybe something more? Gina understood this. She also had some similar experiences with being stopped, as Tommy had been stopped... The thing was that the incidents that were occurring around town were not just "stunt double incidents". It was more of an evil entity. Gina would travel to the local 7-11, sometimes in the evening. And while she drove along the dark, misty roads... she could swear that she observed the walking bodies of the recently deceased. The way they walked, and the sense that was immediately perceived...was one of discomfort.

Something unnatural, something sinister, something that simply was not right. Randy stated: "ARE YOU SERIOUS? Or are have you been watching too many of those area 51 UFO programs!" She laughed, briefly. Gina did love watching programs about government conspiracies...about little green aliens in flying saucers. But, this was different. What was happening was not an alien invasion. There were even rumors around her high school. Gina had heard school staff talking about "strange kids walking around in the late evening". "Strange kids that looked different, walked different and smelled like sea water".

They talked more. Talked for hours and lost track of time. It was okay, they did not have much planned for the weekend. They could sleep late, after they returned to her house – nearly close to 4 AM. The ocean breeze felt good to the skin. The storm had passed and their surroundings were wet. Tommy was wondering if the rumors were true.

Would it be possible to take a dead body and bring it back to life? Biologically, this seemed near impossible. Or was it just improbable, with a small possibility?

In the six months apart, Tommy had seen more of the world than he could have imagined. It was a good thing... It was also a bad thing. He had left the realm of what he knew. He left to experience some wonderful sites, with nice people. He also experienced the cold, harsh darkness of uncivilized worlds. A snap shot of what existed outside the comfort of suburbia, Long Island. Gina smiled at Tommy as he spoke of some of the good experiences. He was nice to her. She was nice to him. Tommy changed gears, in a kind way. He pretty much got right to the "personal" point. It has been six months since our "departure from one another..." I'm heading to the first year of academics, at the University... you are on your way to completing your senior high school year... from what I know and understand [for what it is worth, if you care...] let's do this...[he paused] She looked curious... and she said: "do what?". He continued... take the next five years to sort things out, well, whatever you need to sort out.... I will continue studies at University, with affiliation to the US military... Tommy proposed that they date other people... nothing too serious, just to keep a "healthy human condition". He thought inside that he was not happy with that suggestion to her... but, it was fair. It just was not natural or healthy to expect anyone to not be close to the "human condition".

That is, to kiss – to hug – to love. So, he said: "what do you think? What is the worst that could happen between the two of us, within a five-year period of time?" Silence ensued the car, as the cool ocean breeze blew outside. The silence was broken with her fist grabbing his shirt... She squeezed him and pulled Tommy to her lips. After the deep, passionate kiss... She replied: "NO, WE ARE TOGETHER!".

They snuggled in the car for about an hour after that; it seemed longer [perhaps...it felt like time and space did not exist – just complete happiness]. Tommy was happy that Gina had made it clear to him, clear of her very personal intentions. He was happy that she sealed all the insecurities he had with her...she sealed those insecurities with her strong fist, followed quickly with the softest most sincere kiss Tommy had ever experienced! He knew of the sincerity, it was a gift [or a curse] – depending on how one looked at a person that innately always carried his heart on his sleeve...

It was not just her gentle passionate kiss. Gina displayed incredible qualities. She had similar qualities to the "Basic Instinct" Sharon Stone character...her look, her zest for life...and more. But her soul was pure with an amazing level of brightness, of goodness for her lover. And Tommy...Tommy was a loyal gentleman with an inner wolf like instinct. Tommy was loyal – he had always felt this, deep in his inner core. He did not "sleep around" with many women. The pheromones were always felt and the chances were there – and he was thankful.

It's just that the connections were more "Casanova type" connections. He did connect further...just not with many. The few "deeper intimate connections..." could only be counted on one hand... and on the other hand, a few that were not relationships, just good friendships that went to another level. And that was him, that was Tommy – he loved, he loved where it meant something...So, it killed him to propose to Gina, that they see other people. He had no intention to really "see other people" and maybe "sleep around". No, that was not his style – it never was... It killed him that he was proposing this… It was his way to keep the "connection" with her, while she took the five years to sort out the things [whatever those things were?] she needed to sort out. When Gina put a stop to all this talk…he sighed internally – a complete sigh of "relief".

He just wanted to continue to build the relationship and do all the things that brought her happiness. And she loved sharing the things Tommy enjoyed… That's a good start to a wonderful life!

Tommy spent the week in classes, up at the local University. Gina was finishing classes at her high school. It was senior year, and she had "senioritis". Meaning that she and most other seniors did not want to be there. They had just about finished their requirement to graduate and just wanted to head out into the world! For her, she was leaving the state to study science. The week went by and Tommy found himself at Gina's house early Saturday morning. After cooking an ample amount of egg whites...eating the egg whites, then feeding the yokes to his lab dog "Smokey" he noticed that her fur had grown extremely shiny black.

It must have been due to the many mornings of eating egg yolks! The gym opened at 5AM and he was there to pump the iron. Full leg squats with warm ups at 135 pounds, then 225 pounds. After the warm up, an accelerated weight set with 315 lbs, followed with the final weight set on the gluts...425 pounds. After the final set, Tommy cooled off with the 135 lbs, ten to fifteen reps.

The shower woke him up, it was refreshing. Outside the gym he noticed the oddest weather – snow! It was possible that snow fell in early autumn, but not often on Long Island – since it was surrounded with a warm body of ocean. He carefully drove his rusty car across town to meet Gina. Quietly, he parked his car in front – away from the house. Tip toeing across the front lawn, he jumped on top of the fence – grabbed the roof to hoist himself onto a small ledge. The ledge led to Gina's second story bedroom. Carefully and quietly he moved passed one bedroom window [her brother's]. After that, he reached her window and tapped gently on it. She moved the curtain aside and glanced outside. She had the cutest look, with long smooth silky blond hair all over the place… Gina's sleepy eyes opened wider to see her pretty soft brown trait. The window opened and Tommy rolled into her bed, quietly…

It was early, near 8 AM…everyone is sleeping. Gina just wanted to go back to sleep – it was a SATURDAY! Her mischievous smile communicated something different. She asked Tommy where his bedroom etiquette was?

He had just showered at the gym and had fresh clothes on…he wasn't sure what she meant. She cleared his confusion… let's get bare! And they did… nothing sexual, just a calm quiet sleep together, that morning.

Later that day, the snow fall had reached a record depth. The roads were plowed though and Gina wanted to explore. The rumors of the walking dead were real. She heard that something was happening in a tunnel, that connected a beach with it's car parking lot. So, they headed out – to East Long Island. First, Tommy wanted to quench some need for speed. Tommy and Gina drove to an empty parking lot, slicked over with ice and snow...He made sure her seat belt was buckled...as for him, he endured an incredible amount of risk the previous six months...a seat belt was the last thing on his mind. Within the parking lot, the car was accelerated to a speed of 40 mph, then he slammed on the braked – which started the "spinning of a donuts"! The car moved haphazardly across the parking lot, sliding and stopping with different accelerations

& brakes...It quenched the thrill of the speed!

They caught their breath, smiled and hugged. After that they headed out east to the beach.

The Tunnel

Brian was finishing his shift in the dark, cool, wet tunnel. He noticed two trams [Tram A and Tram B], located across the room as he left. He was a college student that was maintaining some experiment in this dreary place. He reported to a professor at the University. The lab Brian worked in housed coffin like incubators. The incubators really did look like coffins. Rumor had it that there were in fact human bodies in each of the twenty coffins! His job was to just simply take some incubator temperatures and document a few other studies throughout the night. He played some music during his shift, watched television...and other times, just left to take a walk along the beach.

As he left that night, Brian ensured that the exit door was locked...The professor always visited this dark area, a few times each week. He was sinister, with the look to match the personality. Bright as a torch, with regard to knowledge. No inner soul and no ability to love though. The coffins did in fact contain some seaweed soaked dead bodies! The professor grinned at the thoughts of proceeding with the experiments. His area of expertise was "anatomy and physiology". A subject matter that contained five to seven different areas of science: biology, chemistry, immunology, virology, microbiology, neurobiology, application of various techniques/methodologies for experimentation into the UNKNOWN... Surprisingly, he was not that bad of a lecturer! He started lectures with "current events", the happenings of the world. He enjoyed listening to the student's discussion… and he enjoyed the technical questions… he continued his lectures with the use of a chalk board and the use of a power-point presentation. His style was to walk around the room and talk, make eye contact – engage his audience. That all was non-existent in this dark underground bunker, located on a Long Island beach.The professor had two recent successes with his dark experimentation. The success was to transform the "dead" to the "walking dead". There were some complications… The technical considerations were daunting. Even for a fully trained professor, the data collected needed to be "summarized", needed to be "analyzed correctly". To the trained eye, to the subject matter guru, it needed to be a process – defined with critical test parameters. He laughed, listening to the nearby television. A news reporter was attempting to disseminate "data" to the public. He thought: These shitheads could really be responsible for world-wide

PANIC! It was a process that required a "basic understanding" of principles – of concepts. It was a process that required an "in-depth" understanding of those same principles, of those same concepts. And that was the tip of the iceberg (so to speak). What was beneath the water, was an even "DEEPER" understanding of this information – the "pragmatic application..." and that pragmatic application could only be correctly disseminated with "EXPERIENCE".

So, it was a process. The process required two key foundations: (A) knowledge and (B) experience. Through the grace of GOD, the marriage of A to B would provide solutions. The final foundation of this process was the most essential part = THE WISDOM of Great Leadership.

Of course, Professor Brian was not like most professors...He liked the news reporters... He liked that there was little to no ETHICS! And so, he proceeded with his evil experimentation, even if it would have a "DEVESTATING" impact on Long Island!

Gina and Tommy – the love birds 😊

Gina was a true lady. She taught Tommy to be light handed (with some added passion that was just a little more than a light hand), to snuggle... and to value the true genuine meaning of life – living with a real connection, glued with laughter, sincerity... with curiosity for "mystery..." weather it was the mystery of a soul, the mystery of faith – or just a mystery for the supernatural (example = Unidentified Flying Objects, UFOs!).

They drove that evening to the local Long Island Beach. It was a local hang out. A place to catch the rays of the sun, during the day. Or a place to stroll along the sandy beach, in the evening {absorbing the beauty Of a Long Island sunset, and maybe collecting sea shells...} After arriving at the beach, Tommy and Gina parked the car. The car parking lot was empty. It was late, after ten PM. They walked together, through a long dark tunnel, that connected the parking lot to the main part of the beach. About halfway into the tunnel, Gina noticed a bioluminescent light – shining from a sealed door! They stopped in front of the door, with curiosity. Tommy tried to open the door, without success. They didn't think much more of this strange door {no additional thoughts of what could be inside this door} tonight. They would certainly return to this place on another weekend! The beach was nice. Gina collected sea shells and Tommy listened to her talk. He added to the conversation she was having with him. He asked her what had happened when they were apart. She seemed a little distant. He said: its okay, I just wanted to break the ice a bit...he really didn't need the details, unless she wanted to talk about it. He continued, if it's okay – I would like to shed some light to you... about how important you were to me, when we were apart. You see, I never got the chance to talk about those things...he paused for awhile (emotional). Then continued...I didn't get the chance because when I returned to you, everything I knew – just about everything had changed! Change is good, change could be scary... change can be a building force, change can be a destructive force... for me, I came home to great, immediate, devastating sadness. She grabbed his arm, gently – kissing him so passionately (a kiss that offered an unspoken mutual understanding...), he smiled slightly, and she smiled back – with the soft brown eyes of "understanding". Gina asked: "what did you want to say when you came back?". He was so soft spoken, bearing the deep scars of hurt. When I got there, to the military training – I had never been on a plane before – not once in my entire life. I come from humble beginnings, you know that...And on the plane, I was completely hung over! She laughed at him...and said, why in the world would you get drunk the night before you had to head out to military bootcamp. He laughed back... I plead the fifth...truth is, I have no clue! But, I do remember leaving, and that was a tough thing to do – for both of us.

As the plane was landing, through the clouds in Chicago I could see a greenish haze. I was thinking that this seems "supernatural", this seems "odd..." and then I thought, "what the hell did I get myself into". There was no turning back though, and that was okay. I just needed some more water, to neutralize my hangover! On base I survived because of you – you really have no idea. I was lucky, I was thankful to have your love through the training. It was intense, it was brutal – not everyone made it. The level/amount of things a soldier was trained to perform in one day's time was incredibly amazing. The shock upon arrival would always be etched into my soul. They strip you down to nothing, you are nothing – a ground zero state. All your clothes are removed and boxed. The address is typically to mommy and daddy's residence. You stand there bare assed, with no clothes – and you move forward from there to a station to get your government issued shorts.

A t-shirt and shoes followed. And we waited a few days, just like that – until our sister company formed. The training started a day or so after the initial "shock".

Tommy continued to walk peacefully along the ocean with Gina. She listened with a kind arm around his hip. Tommy said: things got better as time moved forward. But, you see it was "total isolation", away from the people you loved. And that was very challenging. A few weeks into the intense training we started receiving mail – in the evenings.

Your perfume letters saved me! Your words were all heart. The country song lyrics you wrote were all heart. The perfume was amazing, and Tommy loved the scent. He sat there reading, thinking that he wished that he could taste this on her soft skin. Tommy could not, though. The training transformed him and everyone that survived. The transformation was from "a civilian" to a "military person". At the end of the training, Tommy finally reached graduation day – with everyone (soldiers crawling to graduation day). In fact, the night before you came to the graduation... his company was brought into a briefing room. Someone in the company fucked something up and pissed off a commander on base. That commander threatened to have our entire company return to the first day of training! To skip graduation and to not see our loved ones! Fortunately, that did not Happen and after the long ceremony... there you were! A memory etched deep in me, I can even see your cute white shirt with dark purple shorts. You have no idea how it is to be in this kind of isolated training, and not be in contact with the one you love. The moment we reconnected, The Moment you hugged and kissed me words cannot accurately describe... anyway, I was frightened that life would have gotten in the way...as life usually does. Everything had changed when I returned to long island – you did not. I just wanted to say "thank you", it meant more to me – more than you will ever know – "hun-bun lick" – they smiled and stopped walking.

In the night sky was a full moon. The ocean was calm, the air was refreshing. Gina and Tommy passionately and gently embraced each other on the beach.

The Seasons Change

The semester was nearing the end. Tommy typically lost ten to twenty pounds during this time. It was extreme intensity... an incredible level needed to be reached, just to survive the waves (upon waves, upon waves...) of academic challenges. The tests were brutal, and in the science arena – it was all cumulative (information from day 1 to the final day of classes). It was not information that could just be "memorized". No. It was information that needed to first be memorized with creative approaches (e.g., the use of acronyms... that helped to remember complex processes...) followed with "the application of the memorized information". And through a variety of "additional strategies", the information was "learned". There was no easy way... the only way to approach it, to prepare for it... was to invest the time, the sacrifice, the hours, the days, weeks, months...just to get to an acceptable level. A level of "survival". The final exams were over, for now.

The holiday season was the nicest time of year for Gina and Tommy – they loved spending time with family, drinking eggnog, decorating Christmas trees... and attending parties! Tommy's mother worked for a Veteran's hospital, in Northport – Long Island. Tommy and Gina were invited to a spectacular Christmas party, in the "Huntington Town House". The place was a symbol of elegance, a beautiful white castle structure. Many weddings happened there and many parties were scheduled...especially with the holiday season. Tommy's family arrived at the party. It was a Saturday evening. The "house" truly was a castle – with pretty white lights on the trees that surrounded the property. Inside was even more spectacular. Grand marble stair cases, brightly lit crystal chandelier's. They followed the signs to their banquet room. Gina and Tommy did not know many people because they were coworkers of his mother's. Tommy's mother was a nursing assistant in the hospital. Her immediate coworkers, friends – were seated at the large round decorated table. Gina and Tommy sat next to some family. The music was an assortment of holiday jingles –

Gina and Tommy came from humble beginnings. Their homes were located in suburbia, eastern long island. So, driving west from Medford to Huntington was exciting to them. Their Christmas party was not the only party that night. Many different holiday parties were scheduled during that time. They could see many different people walking around the castle, through the castle hallways... it was a bit overwhelming for them. But, it was okay. Gina was a down-to-earth lady. She held a proud sense of good southern family roots. Tommy admired the niceness about Gina...the way she presented herself. She was a true family-oriented lady! Her soul was bright, her eyes showed the kindness in her heart. That night Gina was wearing a very pretty velvet dark green dress. In her purse she brought a pair of dark stockings for her legs (just in case the temperature got too cool). They anticipated that the night would be amazing...however, the combination of social pressures – coupled with some added stress... resulted in a "breaking point". Her dress strap broke and she became extremely upset... Tommy's mom had a pin that she gave her to help fix the dress issue...

Tommy and Gina left the great dance hall, and found a very spacious – private dressing room. Gina loved Tommy. Tommy felt the same. They complemented each other. Tommy just wanted to help (if he could). He could see how distressed she was, she had become "emotional". He admired the genuine way about her. She was human and sometimes being human meant that you need help. We rely on one another and when a good couple complements each other – it is a wonderful thing. He was her rock, and although he did not know much about "dress mishaps", Tommy was there as some level of emotional support. Gina would be the first to jump in to help Tommy, if he needed that emotional support to (and he would, we all need that loving support of a soulmate).

His kind words, his assistance with fixing her broken strap with the pin was greatly appreciated. Gina was calm and stared into his eyes... They enjoyed the night's festivities. It was a nice Christmas party, with great music and good food. They met a lot of nice people that worked with Tommy's mom – at the Veterans hospital. They thought it was funny to have a hospital on a road that was called "bread and cheese road". The staff worked various shifts in the hospital, and in different buildings. Some veterans would visit for routine blood work. Others were permanent residents. The government invested a good amount of resources to keep the hospital grounds viable. The investment was appreciated by the staff and helped many warriors. Men and women who returned home, with the battle scars of war (physical and emotional scars). After the party, Gina went home. Tommy would not see her for some time. He was busy with University challenges, and she was finishing her senior year of high school.

It was now another season, just entering spring. Tommy picked Gina up from her part time job at the local Medford McDonalds. He was still in pretty good shape, pumping iron at the local gym – in alignment with military standards. It was Friday evening, and he completed an incredible cardio/weight lifting regiment... he showered, then drove directly to get Gina. As he waited outside the fast food facility, he was getting extremely hungry. He must have burned to many calories... laughing [to himself] and smiling – he realized that it was the end of the McDonalds shift. The place was closing for the evening. That meant any left-over big macs and cheeseburgers were his! Gina loved him and she pretty much was in sync with his thoughts. As she opened the car door, a big bag of left-over burgers first entered the car! She said: "for you: DORK!". She closed the door and smiled at Tommy. He hugged, kissed her – then thanked her for the food. She asked if he could drive the car to the back of the parking lot, he did.

As he was chomping into the first burger, he looked at Gina and said: "you smell like McDonalds!" She laughed. It was true, after working a shift in that place, the aroma of fast food seeped into the clothes. Tommy thought it was cute. She followed conversation: "that is why I brought a change of clothes... and why we are parked in the back of this parking lot". As she changed he clothes, she stopped mid-way. She was teasing him, and he was torn between a cheeseburger and what he admired..." her taste in cute silky front snapped bras!".

The next day was a nice spring morning. Tommy took a day off from the gym. He slept peacefully with Gina, in her full-sized bed. She gently woke him with a moist kiss to the ear. The kiss pierced his ear drum and reached deep into his heart...what a way to wake up! Gina loved the conspiracy theories. She had all the UFO theories figured out. And she was an expert in AREA 51. Today, though, she presented a new conspiracy theory. There was talk about how the sun kept burning...how was it possible that the sun continued to generate life saving beams of light to earth? Gina was bright, she was brilliant... a bit of a science nerd. Her conspiracy theory reached into the realm of religion, with some science fiction. Her theory had to do with soulless evil. Some that walked the earth without souls, with deep dark evil did have a purpose in the ecosystem. Upon their death (departure from the earth), their dark energy went straight to hell. And HELL was the transport to the center of the sun! Tommy looked at this energetic beauty and said: "it is early, give me some time to digest your conspiracy theory...um, and why aren't you wearing a bra?" They exploded in laughter. He knew she was again teasing him. He loved her. She loved him...

Back in the tunnel

The Medford community was a circle of hell. There were a lot of good people. However, the animals of the community also were there and thrived, and were supported with the town and state infrastructure. The evil people of the community were animals. A typical evening, in their homes were filled with violence. Slamming of doors, psychological abuse OF innocent teenage children. Abuse of younger children and even babies. The evil got away with it because they knew that there were not enough laws to protect the children. The children were constantly exposed to excessive violence, excessive animal like behavior, that created a terrible level OF anxiety in the children. The children often complained of having headaches of being anxious, of having stomach issues, trouble digesting food. They were frightened. The evil consisted of females that called themselves "ladies". They were not, in fact they were so far from the "lady", they were not even an animal... they were just pure evil with female parts. The so-called men (evil entities) that followed the evil "ladies" were also psychologically and physically abusive to the children of the community. They would often arrive home and slam doors. That created great anxiety in the children's minds. The children had terrible headaches from the animal-like violence.

The evil "males" just Had male parts. The parts rarely worked correctly. They were plagued with erectile disfunction, with an inability to keep a healthy erection. And perhaps that is why they were so angry all the time... or more like they were just utterly PATHETIC soulless Bodies walking around the community. Most of the people wouldn't care so much, of this evil misery - because of their lack of "wood...". But, it was more than that. The evil were child abusers. They were also MURDERERS!

Dr. Brian was in the tunnel, working on new applications in his experiment. He was working with a formula that utilizes three basic components: Force, Mass and Acceleration. The formula was Force = Mass x Acceleration. The dead bodies were kept frozen, until he could properly infuse the captured dark matter...applying the F=MA formula. His project started with small animals. But he was easily bored with that. In secret, he started with one dead human body. And his formula application worked! He was able to transfer dark matter, into a dead body – and bring it back to life! The body was zombie like though, with some intelligence... Part of the process included infusion of the body tissues with sea water. What Dr. Brian did not realize was that these walking dead bodies were smarter than he calculated. In the light of the moon night, after all staff had left the tunnel...One or two bodies would leave to search for human flesh...

"Love never loses". Tommy had read that somewhere. And he felt and understood the warm impact of its meaning. It was true, for some...maybe. Maybe not. The truth, though, was that sadly "love, sometimes, does lose". There were hundreds of reasons why that could be. No, there were thousands of reasons, or maybe more than that.... And this probably was the single greatest tragedy for the human heart. For the human soul. Especially if the workings of evil had anything to do with the destruction of love. Evil may smile at destruction of this (it is easier to destroy than it is to build. To build requires more brains, more strategy, more capacity to be innovative, etc.) .... But, the natural mechanism, the natural system designed by the love of our creator always found a way... a way to shine a bit of light on the darkness... that was and will always be a comfort to the broken hearted.... To all those souls impacted by the workings of malicious darkness....

The time apart scared Tommy the most. Tommy felt that if time apart was necessary, then so be it. For example, studies in another state, service to country (his experience...) were all reasonable circumstances for being apart from his soulmate... the distance and time apart brought increased risk that life would, possibly, wedge an unscalable wall between these lovers. And even if one heart made it past the wall life had built during time apart.... The other heart may not have been so lucky.... One heart may have been impacted in such a way that there was no way to scale the wall of life... and that was one of the thousands of examples for the sad reality/the true meaning of the statement: "love sometimes does lose".

Tommy asked with a quiet voice "how do we take what we have, take it to the next level"? What do you call me, when other people ask you (and, I am not around)? Am I your boyfriend?

Are we exclusive? Are we intimate with one another (will we be?) Is there good intent to hopefully one day soon.... Sleep over at one another's homes? If there is no answer to these questions.... Then what are we? Where are we? Are we in a relationship? Who would you spend Valentine's night with? When my birthday comes, will you share a bottle of wine with me sometime during my birthday weekend? Would you want to sleep over and just cuddle with me through the night? If the answers are not clear.... Then, what are we? Am I confused or am I your loving boyfriend....?

Gina's father was a good dad to her. He allowed her to grow together with Tommy. Over the years...Tommy thought that perhaps it was the qualities her father saw in him. Tommy was loyal, he cared for Gina...and most importantly he could see that his daughter cared immensely for Tommy. They made each other smile, they share laughter, they enjoyed doing little to nothing. Even simply enjoying the sun shine on a Saturday afternoon was exciting, showered with beams of love. Tommy sensed that Gina's father could see their genuine love.

It was a good way...allowing his daughter to experience the happiness of a relationship...even if it meant that she would be in love with another gentleman [her first love would still always be with her dad...].People could be cruel sometimes. Probably cruel intent was more common than many wanted to believe. Gina came across some cruel souls (or soulless people) during her high school years...and would meet similar shitheads in her college years. Tommy offered a rationale, calm, peaceful love to her...and would always be there for her. Tommy understood that there were bad characters out there, that had no niceness about them. The locker room talk was sometime an eerie reminder of these types of evil. No sense of moral, no sense of decency. The locker room was an interesting place for this type of talk. Tommy was a shy guy...he exhibited a traditional soul. He always felt deeply that some things should remain private. Brad was a shit head on one of the sports teams. Tommy shared locker room space with him... Brad was a player with the women and he was good at it (in a sinister way). Brad often bragged about his encounters with a local red head girl.... Her style... and what she did behind closed doors. For Tommy, he had the gift of seeing through the bullshit.... it was a gift, and a curse....

In this shithead "Brad's" eyes were a devilish level of exaggeration about the red head girls sexual abilities...and Tommy felt the sadness. For him, sadness that anyone would feel the need to brag... unless it just was not true. And even if some of this shithead's locker room chat had some truth...Tommy thought that Brad should consider himself extremely lucky to have connected with such a good lady like soul. That night, Tommy and Gina snuggled while watching corny MTC rerun movies. Gina liked those kind of movies...like the rocky horror picture, sixteen candles, mystic pizza ...the body guard. The movies brought her happiness. And Tommy was always happy for her.... Her good soul deserved pure happiness in a (sometimes) cruel world....

The Walking Dead: not the experiment Gina and Tommy stumbled upon.... no something else, "the training accident in the middle of the Atlantic..."

There had been a sinister experiment being performed, right in the bowels of Long Island. The experiment was secret and it was funded with blood money. And as progress was made with the experiments, a group of "monsters" were created. The mysterious deaths that had occurred on Long Island was just the tip of the ice berg. Gina suspected it and she even observed some familiar faces walking in the moonlight. It frightened her. Tommy being back in town was a comfort to her. They were back together. She was happy to share her love with him. It seemed to have been too long a time, to not have connected genuinely with her soul-mate. She had loved others….but, was it true love? The love was there, the connection was partial.

Tommy slept over, in Gina's warm embrace. They spent most of the night awake – talking. She was a great story teller. He admired her conspiracy theories. Tommy wished that the sinister experiment she spoke about was also just a conspiracy theory. It was not a conspiracy. The town was evil. The surrounding towns were evil. She knew it. He guessed that he had known it for some time. Tommy just did not want to believe it. Tommy was designed to always see the good in people. To see the good in town. There was not much good to see in Patchogue, New York. There was not too much good to see in the surrounding areas. It was sad. Sad because although that was just the way it was…there were good souls. Gina was one of the good souls.

She always shined brightly to who ever was lucky enough to share her light. And the evil experiments created the unthinkable. The evil monsters that walked in the moonlight. The dead that lived for short periods of time. They were preying on their victims... and, it was typically a violent gruesome scene. She left the bedroom for a short time, then strolled back into the room, in an elegant way. Tommy immediately realized the scent of her lady perfume. It brought him to a state of euphoria. As she crossed the room in her soft cotton pajamas, she passed the bed where Tommy was. She walked across the room to turn off her desk lamp light. As Gina turned toward the path of the desk light, Tommy could see that her pajamas were seductive. Below her waist, behind her – was skin. The pajamas were pulled down to reveal her soft skin. The light went out and Gina quickly snuggled into bed with Tommy. They were incredible lovers. It was not just physical. There was a complete connection. A rare connection of the souls. They could hear howling in the air outside. Tommy and Gina continued to snuggle and talk, later into the early morning hours.

Gina was curious about the abilities she had noticed. It was him, and it was more... She asked what had happened to him while they were apart for the six months. He breathed deeply and spoke softly. Tommy spoke slowly, with a perceived respect for the "unknown powers". Gina was intrigued, since she was an expert in the "conspiracy theories". Tommy wished he could confirm that what he spoke of was conspiracy. He continued.... Deep in the ocean, there are things you would not believe.

Most people might believe, but not fully understand. Even the trained soldier had trouble believing some of it. It was a dark night, a stormy night. Just before you had called to ask for some company at the Patchogue funeral.The missions have and have always had inherent risks. Training accidents happened all the time. No one heard much about the details of training accidents. It was dark, the equipment was working well. The first part of the exercise was to drop 200 feet, quickly into the turbulent ocean abyss. As you head into a free fall, into water – hitting the surface is critical. You hit the surface the wrong way and your bones break...it is that simple. Heading into the ocean that night was not easy. There were multiple training accidents. Many did not survive. She stopped him, and asked why in the world they would train for that. He smiled, briefly then hugged her. Softly, Tommy spoke: "train for the worst, train in the harshest environments... under the most hellish conditions... and hope not to ever have to engage in use of the skills". However, the skills were historically used in various war-time situations...often.

Tommy stopped smiling. He addressed Gina's concern for the walking monsters. They needed to be stopped and they would be. What they did not realize, was that the person who returned to this place, also was "the walking dead". He felt he was a monster – in some ways. In other ways, a gift to continue on...for as long as the creator allowed him time on this Earth. Gina grabbed him, "I knew you were different, you seemed more electrical though – full of an incredible energetic life".

He was brought back from the cold dark Atlantic ocean abyss. The life was brought back, as he travelled briefly into the afterlife. He was shy to talk about the next part of his "walking dead story". Gina was intrigued. Tommy said he needed to suck blood from humans. And she moved into him, within a heart-beat. Tommy gently inserted his grip and sucked. The connection between monster and lady, not only provided a sustained life for Tommy. Gina immediately noticed an electrical energy within her own body!

The End (continued in chapter 2)

2

Evil Returns

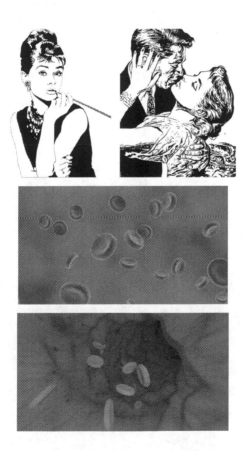

Time passed. Time passed too fast – as it usually does... It was another weekend together. Tommy and Gina enjoyed long walks on the Long Island beaches. They would sometimes collect the most unique types of sea shells. Other times they would just enjoy the sound of the ocean and the scent of the fresh breeze. Gina was always so curious.... She wanted to know more about Tommy. After the first exchange of blood, she felt more alive. Gina felt stronger with a heightened awareness for all her "senses". Her sense of sound, of sight, of taste all were incredibly sensitive to her surroundings. Tommy smiled at her, and said: "be careful what you wish for, you just might get it...".

She was a conspiracy guru, and she wanted to know all that was not spoken about. Tommy loved the thrill of the training, the challenge of the hunt. In the middle of the Atlantic Tommy lost his life. Gina stopped him. "what do you mean, lost your life...? Like, you died?". Pretty much, that's about it. Dead, no life = just a piece of meat with nothing to steer the biological processes. You see, though, I was brought back. For me, it seemed like no time had passed. Tommy looked into the ocean distance...months had passed, but to me it was instantaneous! What happened...what really happened... I don't know for sure. But, death is death.

On the ship, in the medical area – all shattered leg bones were replaced with a type of metal. A strong metal. The legs are hybrid with the live body. The thing is... he paused. Sorry, just some physiology... Tommy asked if she minded hearing about human anatomy and physiology? She smiled and replied: "be careful what you wish for...". Of course! He continued: The center of the bones is where one of the most important biological process takes place. A continuous supply of fresh red blood cells. The red blood cells are circulated in our blood, and they carry oxygen throughout our body. The same red blood cells also transport the carbon dioxide after the oxygen has been used in our bodies. Every sixty or so days, there is complete replenishment of the red blood cells. This happens in the center of the bones. My bones are strong now, with the capability to lift 1500 pounds. I don't usually lift that weight. More like a 700 to 800 pounds weight lifting regiment gives me a good pump! And doesn't cause to much "attention". The trade-off if, though, is that I can not generate red blood cells. That is why I must feed on your blood!

Gina said: "you can suck on me anytime!" Tommy laughed! I would like that. To continue to be living (or the walking dead...), I would need at least a 30 to 60 day feeding. There is more to the physiology. It's not just that, there was a transplant of energy into my core. And the energy runs through the "artificial circulatory system". The energy increases the basic animal instincts. You feel any increase in your animal instincts? She grabbed him and tackled Tommy to the ground! They loved passionately.... Animal enough for you? They just relaxed and smiled. It was a new world and they were in love...they were happy.

"The Evil Returned and Could Not Be Contained"

The professor, Dr. Brian returned to the tunnel. It was a cold dark night in the middle of winter. He drove across two long bridges and eventually reached the parking lot of this haunted Long Island beach. He had not planned to stay too late. The experiment was running well, and he just needed to take some measurements...after all, it was a Friday evening. Even an evil professor had plans at the start of a weekend! Dr. Brian walked cautiously from the large parking lot, into the tunnel – taking note of a family of deer grazing in the distance. The dark tunnel was long and connected the open parking lot to the ocean. About halfway into the tunnel was a rusty, locked door. The professor opened the door and stepped into the corridor. He quickly closed and locked the door behind him. A good twenty-minute walk in a dimly lit hallway was next. The professor carefully walked as the cement walkway was narrow...and descended abruptly at times. The tram A and tram B experiments were sealed, in an "inactive state". He dared not touch those botched experiments. He heard that there was some curse associated with each tram. And, the professor did not want to explore a cursed tram!

Researching dead bodies was more of his "style". The coffins were locked and the bodies inside were alive, "so to speak". The measurements were significant. The experiments were working. He believed that the "dead" would be walking very efficiently, very soon...He closed the books, ensured that all the incubators were operational. One last check of the coffins, then he headed out the door to start the weekend. The lab was quiet as the first coffin opened. The body of a recently deceased boy exited. This was not the first time the walking dead left the laboratory. Late at night, when the lab was empty, the walking dead left to search for human flesh. The body was there, it was semi-functioning. Sort of a zombie state, with some intelligence. And carnal thirst for human flesh and blood. The soul and heart were not present. This body, Mark, was not "Mark". This body was infused with an evil energy. The energy was scientifically infused into his anatomy and physiology.

The walking dead found his way off the beach...into a northern Long Island Community. His appearance was dark, with a black hood covering his face. The clothes he wore were "presentable" and he was semi-intelligent. Mark found his way to the local bus, and late in the evening he was near a "duck pond" in St. James, Long Island.Kristen was babysitting this cold winter's evening. It was Friday night and she invited her boyfriend over to the St. James mansion. Her boyfriend had recently completed a law degree and was taking on various legal cases. However, within a few months of practicing law on Long Island, he sadly lost his license. The bar association revoked his law license since he committed various unethical crimes. One included the spending of a retainer, before the services were even started. The mansion was incredible and somewhat "eerie".

The house was big and the hallways were lit very dimly. Outside was a full moon. The cold breeze blew against the house and added to the eerie noises. Many strange sounds were heard inside the house and Kristen was happy that her boyfriend finally arrived, near midnight.

The long driveway was steep, then dropped into a "valley". At the final part of the driveway, the house stood – and it was a site to see...colonial style, with a detached garage. Stan nearly slid into the house, as his car caught slick ice – about halfway down the driveway. Luckily, the car stopped with enough space between the house and the front bumper!

The children were asleep. Kristen was sleeping over, in the guest room. The parents were out of town. The house was isolated on a twenty - acre plot of deeply forested land. The home was built in a "valley". Not too far from the house, a duck pond was iced over. A narrow, graveled dirt road led up into the development of five or six houses. Stan was complaining about almost sliding off the damn road as he entered the house. He was a miserable son of a bitch. Kristin blamed it on his upbringing. His father had been a violent, abusive alcoholic. He beat the shit out of him, most weeks.

Kristen felt bad for him. Sadly, history followed Stan. He was abusive toward his girlfriend Kristin. They sat in the living room, watching television – as the dark cool wind blew outside. Kristen thought she heard something moving outside the living room window...it was probably the tree branches pushing in the wind. The snow and ice storm started later that night...It would be difficult to drive up the icy driveway in this type of storm; especially with the design of the grounds...

Lunch with the University Researchers

Gina had some connections with five lady researchers [Tommy knew one lady. She was enrolled in a class with him at the University]. Tommy and Gina drove to the University to meet for lunch. The meeting's purpose was to fuel Gina's desire for "conspiracy theories". The ladies worked with Professor Brian, at the University. They also spent time in a secret laboratory, located in a Long Island Beach Tunnel.

The ladies were extraordinary. They each brought with them a passion for excellence. The first, Carmen greeted Tommy and Gina. She had crystal blue eyes that could cut through a gem. Her blonde hair matched her energetic aura. The second lady, Sharon showed an amazing electrical charge. Her silver blue eyes stopped Tommy in his tracks. Matched with a cute athletic blonde pony-tail, for her silky hair. The third lady was named Scarlet. Her appearance was "Gothic", exhibiting mysterious tattoos on her skin (the one Tommy and Gina could see). Her dark red, shiny hair was long. The hair was thick and strong, with sexy curls. Her lips were soft and plump in appearance. As she spoke, Tommy was stunned by how she moved her tongue, quickly out of the corner of her mouth. Scarlets eyes told a story – they were green and light brown in color, deep to anyone who dared look into them. Michelle was a Spanish beauty, with dark pretty eyes and dark curly hair; her appearance was also athletic. Her eyes showed kindness. And finally, the fifth lady: Ivana. She was amazing! She presented the research project goals to Tommy and Gina. Tommy wasn't listening because he was lost in her inviting brown soft eyes, and golden hair.Gina wanted to know more about the research project and she listened to Ivana speak... They were fascinated about the research goal...and also frightened with some of the findings...Tommy proposed that they take a break from the conspiracy theories and the evil experiment. He was hungry and the University had a great selection of "diverse food". There were visiting student from around the world: Russia, China, Japan, India, Ireland... The food was a good comfort to the students. The food was authentic. It was delicious! As they ate their dinner, the researchers that could speak Russian, were joking around [Tommy suspected, from their smiles and laughs...the smiles looked devious to him... these women were great researcher, but they also had a mischievous side...]. It was Friday evening and that meant there would be a party, some were on campus. The plan was to visit the beach tunnel on Saturday night. Friday nights were reserved for "socialization". Even geeky researches needed some free time to listen to punk rock, drink too much beer and... do other things.They all agreed to meet in Ivana's dorm room, since it was a sweet. She shared it with Carmen and Scarlet. There was plenty of space for a dorm "party". There was plenty of space for a "sleep over". They also agreed that if they listened to enough alternative punk rock, drank enough beer...they would increase their creativity! That was the theory, anyway! And even if it didn't work, they would have a lot of fun trying!

Tommy and Gina had a stash of bud light (a pretty good supply), and agreed to meet up with the researches in an hour...

It was about 1 AM on a Friday evening. Kristin was sick and tired of Stan's abuse. Luring him into the "babysitting" sleep over was perfect. Stan sat in the living room, drinking a case of beer – bitching and moaning, still about almost sliding his car into the house. The fucking ice and the steep decline of this driveway is a recipe for disaster. Kristin quietly walked behind him, and gently placed two concentrated drops of a potent liquid poison on his neck. The poison immediately seeped through the skin and made its way to his heart. Tachycardia caused him to drop his beer, spilling it all over the living room rug. The poison did not kill him, just placed him into a state of shock. Kristin reluctantly went over to his side and helped him back onto the couch. She followed with a glass of cool water and baby aspirin. He took the aspirin, and drank the cool water. Stan thanked her for looking after him.

Outside, the cool breeze knocked the tree branches into the side of the house. The sounds startled Kristen and Stan. What they did not realize was the monster lurking at the end of the driveway. The walking dead experiment made his way down the iced driveway, to the side of the house... It was late, and they were watching television in the large living room. Behind the couch they were resting on was the open, dark hallway that led into a modern styled kitchen. Kristen thought she heard something drop in the kitchen area. Stan was back to drinking, and reluctantly agreed to head into the kitchen. Not to check on the sound... more to refill his stiff drink. The kitchen had an island where the hard liquid was located... Stan entered the kitchen, drunk and arrogant...he almost did not realize what was standing beside him, the monster. Stan, the arrogant abusive son of a bitch did not flinch... fools don't usually react to danger – not the way they should. Stan was a tough guy, after all – he could beat on Kristin. He could use his law training to cause chaos and destroy lives (when his law license was not revoked for amoral/unethical behavior...) The monster grinned at Stan, as he stood in the dimly lit kitchen. Monsters are real, heaven and hell are true. Stan was amoral – he did not believe in any of it. All he knew was that "he was a tough guy". Monsters are real and the one that stood in his path was beyond comprehension. In an ironic way, the monster would take care of what should have been taken care of a long time ago. Some things are just above the law, and most people understood that. And the day came when an obscene force removed another piece of societal sludge.

The monster was semi-intelligent... and had an interesting view on human anatomy. He thought: The ligaments and tendons around the knee cap fascinated his animal instinct. He wondered how the flesh in that area of the body would taste. The attack was instantaneous, swift to the victim. Stan's right knee cap was crushed with the monster's forceful kick. The knee, the bone and surrounding support were smashed into the back of his leg. There was no time for a yell, as the first blow was followed quickly with a chunk of flesh being removed from the front of Stan's throat. They both fell to the ground, and the creature fed... The meat surrounding the knee cap was good for this beast. The cap of the knee is the "patella". The Beast ripped off the bony cap and brought it back with him. Sort of a prize. The semi-intelligent monster found his way back to the beach tunnel, just prior to the sun rising over the ocean.

The night at "University" was much more enjoyable than an encounter with a flesh-eating beast. Tommy and Gina parked their car on campus. The University was not too far from the St. James duck pond. The dorms were located in different parts of the University grounds. Although it was very dark, the campus had plenty of light along the ample walking paths. In fact, some walkways were not only lit by the surrounding lights, but also had biologically designed "bioluminescence trees". The trees offered a soft yellow-green glow to the campus night air. After following the signs to the dorms, Tommy and Gina reached their destination. Inside the dorm, they could hear a few parties...

but, mostly the campus was quiet this Friday evening. There were some reasons for the still surroundings: the campus was filled with commuters. That meant that a large population of students did not live on campus, they travelled from local (and not so local) towns to attend classes during the week. On weekends, they were back in their Long Island towns. That did not mean that there was no life on campus, during the weekends... There were plenty of students that did live on campus...and there were also plenty of social gatherings... Parties for the average student were essential. Really needed, to keep the sanity. Balancing the rigorous challenges was one thing. Finding time for some fun was another. Partying was never a priority... but was essential to the four to five-year experience. The researchers knew that the parties were to be kept within reason. That is to say, once or twice a week was reasonable. Any parties that exceeded this would certainly result in flunking out of "University".

Gina had a good friendship with the researchers, and hoped to join the University after her graduation from high-school. Tommy was already there, one year ahead of Gina. The sweet was had nice square footage, for a dorm. There was a nice sized living room and two bedrooms. The bedroom each had bunk beds. The sweet could house four to six students. The party had already started. The music was good – a mixed style of reggae, pop and alternative rock… The beer was there…Tommy added to the stock pile. It was a nice way to spend a Friday evening.

The plan was to enjoy the night, drink the refreshments…listen to the music… play some adult style games (with innocent fun). There was no interest in discussing "science". There were plenty of sleeping bags in the living room. Plenty of water, plenty of snacks, a few pizzas and of-course...plenty of beer.Ivana, being the natural leader that she was, lead the party. And even though science was not on the agenda, all attendees of the party had an interest in what was really being researched at the Long Island Beach tunnel! They had their fill of beer and the "ice was broken" (so to speak). Tommy felt like he had known these researchers his whole life, even though they had only recently met. And this was true...why not, wasn't it possible that a soul or group of souls could have crossed paths some other time, some other place? They sat Indian style, in a circle – listening to Ivana speak to the "secret experiment". The science was fascinating. Was it possible that such experiments existed? To bring back the dead... to some how infuse life into a dead body... was that possible? And she continued to speak about biological theory, application of theory... the layout of the beach lab...

As Ivana spoke with passion, with curiosity, with excitement...Tommy thought. [there was a familiarity with these young researcher ladies...he thought that this small circle of friends would become more than friends... a life-long pack of family... there was just something about each one of these "friends", and it was not the buzz from the beer... he knew how to control his craving for beer (sort of) – and even in the most drunken state, the inner core of thought remained untouched by the alcohol... usually]. Ivana voiced her concern of the ethics. There really was no ethical oversight for the secret beach experiment. The lead researcher was amoral, without much aptitude for medical ethics. Tommy was enrolled in a medical ethics course at University. Ivana attended the class with him. It was a good course, sociology. He thought he would have pursued the sociology field of study... if biological sciences did not exist. The course covered ethics of science. It would continue through the semester, and end with ethics in the hospital setting (since most students were going on to enroll in medical school programs). The do not resus. (DNR) would be covered, later in the semester. Ivana was not lecturing...No, this was a party. She went off on some tangent, laughed and chugged some beer, chugged a lot of beer! The music was good and the company got silly...a good type of silly... a more comfortable atmosphere ensued! Ivana brought a table and some ping pong balls. Filled two large red cups with beer and placed the full cups at each end of the table. Two teams were formed. One team would bounce a ping pong ball on the table, trying to get it to bounce into the beer filled cup. Another turn would follow with the other team bouncing their balls to the other side of the table, with the goal of getting it into the other beer filled cup, Pretty cool game – with one added twist... with every try and "miss of the ball entering the beer filled cup", a piece of clothing would be removed from a team member!

They were not sure how far the game would go, before it was stopped...but, they really did not care. It was fun just being there, talking, laughing and enjoying the party... it was "good innocent fun". As the game continued, Ivana talked more of the beach experiment. Tommy was fascinated...[He thought to himself, she had a way of expression, a way of communicating the dullest topics in the most exciting way... Tommy had some family scars, and at one Point thought He would never want to start a family...Ivana changed his thinking in a heart-beat...the energy that surrounded Her, the ability to light up the darkest areas with Her radiance.... He thought that she would be a great friend, a great mother, a great lover, great at anything she put her mind too. The type of lady that would never hurt her Tommy, never hurt her lover. The type that would never put her lover, Tommy in a position where at a hospital delivery room, an evil conversation would take place to debate changing the name of a soon to be born baby boy.... Things happened in life, sometimes for the better. Sometimes for the worse.... she was divine and although Tommy did not know her _ he trusted her instinct. He believed that she would guide him well. Never hurt Him. Never put him in an evil situation. He did not know why he envisioned sitting in a hospital waiting room, waiting for a baby boy to be born. He was surrounded by evil soulless "people". And these people (family) talked about the legality of changing his soon to be son's name! you could imagine the pain endured... and in His vision the baby boy was born healthy (luckily)... with some perceived distress during delivery, the heart rate of this baby boy dropped significantly lower than what

RICHARD A. BOEHLER, JR.

it should be, a baby in womb showed a fast heart rate...this was healthy, this was normal...In Tommy's vision, the baby boys Heart rate dropped to below sixty beats per minute...and he then pleaded with the doctor to do something...the doctor delivered this healthy baby boy via C-section. However, the vision was followed by more serious circumstances... in His vision he continued to see more....

Tommy left the hospital to get things ready for the baby boys homecoming. He bought a big wooden poster board of a bird with a baby picture and placed it in the front yard. The baby boy would not be allowed to come home too see his dad for almost three weeks! due to some psychotic circumstances surrounding the evil... you could imagine the distress, the pain... something that stabs right to the human heart of a new parent....] and then the vision disappeared.

Tommy returned to the party, was again presented with the beer and pong balls. They were losing THE Game and He was losing his clothes. The party continue until most were not clothed with much. It was okay, they were close friends and they were HAPPY, excited.... They fell asleep together in the living room. Close with one another, cuddling together, Happy, feeling safe (it was a nice Friday evening...). It was a Saturday morning, a cool morning. The campus was empty, with the exception of local student residents. Tommy was an early riser, even when he had a good amount of alcohol in his system the night before. He showered, changed his clothes – then planned to go for a morning walk. First, he kneeled next to Gina and kissed her gently on the forehead. She smiled, and curled back into the blanket. The rest of the ladies were asleep. He quietly left the dorm and walked across campus. The ground was covered with a layer of ice. The trees were bare of leaves. It was winter. The air was crisp and refreshing to his morning senses. Even though the University was less active on the weekend [since it was more of a "commuter college"], there were some events... social gatherings, sports, study sessions... a bakery... Tommy found the University bakery. He purchased enough coffee for every lady. He liked the fresh, warm raspberry cheese scones. Tommy purchased a dozen fresh scones for the dorm. On his way back to Gina, he was thinking about the plans for visiting the secret beach laboratory. They were going to visit the "tunnel lab" [as it was called] later in the day (in the evening). When he got back to the dorm, some were just starting to wake... others were still sleeping. Gina gravitated quickly toward the coffee and scones.

There seemed to be an unspoken energy in this circle of researchers. A magical link between the souls...not like the soulless vampires you read about.... The energy was summoned from hundreds [perhaps thousands] of years – historical triumph, historical failures…this lead to a deep, good-hearted understanding. The bond would certainly continue with these souls – in this life and into the next. In this very circle, they would feed, they would nurture each other – they would love and care for their linked hearts and linked souls. This would bring happiness. This would bring many days of smiling and laughing… and as they travelled the various paths together – they would fight and defeat evil on Earth… they would fight and defeat evil together. Gina, Tommy and the circle of researchers would always be there for each other…. Not one soul would ever feel the pain of "saying good-bye". The pact of angelic vampires would eternally thrive.

Tommy enjoyed the fresh scone and hot coffee. They relaxed quietly together. [Tommy thought: he was lucky to have been in a few great relationships. He wasn't the one to brag. He did not need to, because he knew two things – 1. Although there were only one hand full of women he had been with, in close intimate relationships (less than five…) The time together helped nourish his soul and the soul of his lovers. He was thankful for that…2. He knew…he believed… that if a woman also believed he was "the one", she would not hesitate…she would not risk losing a "true love…" She would claim what was hers…]. Tommy was enrolled in a sociology class with one of the researchers (Ivanka). The class was an elective. A fascinating course entitled "marriage in the family". The theories presented in the course could certainly be applied to real life. The professor lectured of "a funnel theory…" In the relationship, they would start at the top rim of the funnel – swimming freely, with an interest in searching for true love. As they swam through the funnel waters, they would relax and enjoy wooing. The waters were calm and flowed slowly in this area of the funnel. As time passed, the lovers would swim deeper into the funnel waters. They noticed that at the top of the funnel, there were many areas to "leave". Not that they wanted to leave, it was just part of the sociology professor's "theory". And it made sense, a common sort of sense. Where at the early stages of a relationship, there were many "exit points", with less emotional connectiveness. With love, some love. Love that was at the initial area of the relationship – just prior to full bloom and exponential growth.

Tommy day dreamed, as he sipped his hot coffee and enjoyed pieces of the fresh scone. He thought more of the sociology lecture. The funnel theory could be applied to his relationship with Gina. He had been sucked deep into the funnel and reached the "inflection point". A place that most people could not come back from. The area of the funnel that is inflection, has a quick flow of water.

The water essentially sucks water from the large funnel top area into another area…deep below – a changing point. Tommy had given up on Gina, six months had passed and he knew that there was no "going back". Then, in his day dream – he looked up through the clear water. It was Gina above him, swimming gracefully in a fluorescent yellow-green bikini. Her bikini displayed many strings…that were tied to hold her top and bottom together. Her swimming was graceful and beautiful, with elegance. As Tommy reached the inflection point [the point of no return], the strings of Gina's bathing suit unraveled – quickly reaching Tommy. The strings wrapped him and pulled him away from that part of the funnel, immediately toward Gina. As he reached her, they connected – flush with bare skin, wrapped in luminescent string. Together, they exited the funnel… Tommy was nudged by Gina, she asked how his coffee was. He returned to the dorm, and smiled at her. Gina sat next to him and snuggled close to his warmth. It was a good morning... the rest of the researchers were waking and following the scent of fresh coffee.

Saturday night, the researchers were scheduled to work a short shift at the tunnel laboratory. The plan was to meet on the beach, with the essentials = fire wood, beach chairs, and beer. Tommy and Gina would stay by the beach campfire, while some of the researchers worked their shift. Afterwards, they would all meet in the laboratory to take a closer look at what was going on... And it was a nice night, with the cool ocean breeze. The researchers were busy in the lab while Tommy and Gina enjoyed some beer near the campfire. She was wearing a string bikini, and it was the cutest thing Tommy had ever seen. Seductive with an innocent nature [he thought]. It was the string. The string that held it all together. What a fashion style. What a way to spend an evening [lost in thought]. His thoughts did not last too long thought. Gina was playful, and Tommy loved that about her. She challenged him to a beer pong game. The goal of the game was to get the ball in the cup of beer. Bounce it on the table [a piece of beach ply wood they found] and get it in the cup of beer. What was more intriguing to Tommy was what Gina suggested... If he got the ball into the cup, she would let him gently pull a little bit of the bikini string... And the game began, it was a good game. [Tommy realized, as he was bouncing the balls – that he did not suggest anything in return...mutual kisses would be nice – and he would return to her with soft gentle kisses]. The night went by so fast, too fast – as often happens when souls are enjoying themselves... The string was pulled a good distance, and it continued to intrigue Tommy.... Just then one of the researches returned to get

Tommy and Gina. They left the beach to search for clues in the tunnel lab...

Saturday Night in
The Tunnel Lab

They left the beach and entered a dark, dimly lit tunnel. About halfway through the tunnel Tommy, Gina and Ivanka reached the entrance. The door was locked. Ivanka unlocked the door with her key and entered first. After closing and relocking the door, they made their way through a series of dark corridors – using flash lights for guidance. It was an eerie, damp passageway. Finally, they reached the main corridor that lead into the central research lab. Tommy and Gina listened to Ivanka speak to the other researchers. She was curious about the transport module, located at the back of the room. Apparently, there was a rumor that a formula had been practically applied to bring energy from the distant "Sun" into the research lab! Ivanka wasn't sure of the purpose, but had heard that there was a legend of "dark energy" leaving soulless humans, that somehow would find its way to the closest ball of heat – the sun. Some thought it was "hell". Others thought it was nonsense. Ivanka and the researchers were intrigued by the rumors. The formula they came across was for distance. A calculation to send energy through space in time, which was governed with known metrics. Time, acceleration, force, with constants were applied to formula. Gina asked why there were coffins in the lab? And there were incubators that in fact had dead human bodies in them! The thing was, that no one really knew the extent of the real research projects. The college student researchers were only there to gain some cash – which helped buy school supplies in the semester. Their role was to just monitor some basic temperature readings and prepare some basic lab equipment for the professor. The hours sucked, but the shifts were only one to two hours in length. The cash helped with their academic goals... Most of the coffins were solid metal, that had temperature and pressure gauges on the outside doors.

Except for one coffin. Gina stood near the one coffin that showed a clear glass window, in the front door. She peered into the coffin with curiosity. Gina raised her voice to Ivanka, who was located across the room. Is there supposed to be a body in this coffin? Ivanka said "YES". The body was missing...

Gina was savvy, when it came to investigating the unknown. She had a gift and an interest in the unknown. Especially unidentified flying objects... Her goal was to visit area 51 and find out what was really in the underground bunkers. The body was missing and it was walking the streets of local Long Island towns. As the researchers looked through more of the technical literature that night, the walking body roamed into a nearby home. The home of a dentist. The dentist was just finishing the final touches after drilling deep into a molar tooth. After drilling deep into the connective tissue, the bone... he implanted a bit of radioactive isotope. A perfect crime to commit. No one in the community would suspect that the patient would develop "cancer" and that the real cause was due to the radioactive element! The dentist had ties to the local Long Island community. A bunch of shit heads. No, more than just the typical bag of garbage shit head. It's not a crime to walk around smelling like a shit head! However, make no mistake about it... they were criminals. Murderers, in fact. And there was no statute of limitation on discovering/convicting these community linked murderers... In time (sooner or later) the criminal would meet their justice (in this life or the next...).

Directly or indirectly. There were ties to criminal activity in the community. It was how they survived. It was how they were able to purchase nice homes in communities that were surrounded by beautiful ocean water. One catch though. Sometimes, people (enemies of the NY state) needed to be "taken out". Not cold-blooded murder, there wasn't much sport in that... it needed to be more of a game, a game of chess for the criminal minds. There were contacts in the local hospitals, there were contacts in dental offices. Routine colon screenings became opportunities to implant cancer causing cells in men that were on the "target list". Routine tooth drillings were opportunities to implant a cancer-causing agent...deep into the base of the tooth. Months later, a cancer would develop... blood borne cancer, lymphoma was the typical result. The patient left the dental office, in pain. The doctor was cleaning up the dental procedure mess, when the walking corpse arrived in his house.It's interesting to see the behavior of a criminal that meets up with a cold-blooded murdering corpse. There isn't much fear, why would there be? The Long Island community gave these shit heads the "golden key" to society. They were what Long Islanders called "the best doctors!". Yeah, the best double agents! Soulless walking pieces of meat, with a crooked smile. There was no conversation, of course. A swift blow to the side of the head – followed with a precise extraction of the dentists eye ball ended his life. The walking dead took a liking to the juicy consistency of the human eye. It was tasty. Crunching into the eye with his teeth resulted in the pop and splash of eye ball juice, clear across the room. Disgusting to see, if anyone else had been present to witness it. The dentist was alone that night he met the walking dead...

The researchers were reading through some manuals, located on the desk of Professor Brian. The manuals were technical in nature. The lead research, Ivanka, breezed through the literature. There were numerous formulas to decipher. She quickly read the work and concluded that there must be another place in the laboratory. A place where particles were sent to travel long distances, in a circle. One set of particles would be sent through a large circular tube, the size of a football field (if it were circular and not rectangular). The other set of particles were moved in the opposite direction. Following the technical notes, Ivanka clapped her hands together – loudly. This represented the point were all particles, after traveling the complete circle – reached a "smashing point". Gina asked "why in the world would he want to do that?" Ivanka smiled and quickly responded: to create anti-matter (sort of a earthly black hole!). This was different though. Reading through the manuals, it was clear that the impac of the particles created an energy that was needed to propel a transport car along nano-tubule tracks. Tracks that led straight from the tunnel they were in, to a station – hovering in the outer atmosphere. Ivanka wasn't sure why there would be a transport to this "space station". First, they wanted to find the next area of the lab. Searching around the dimly lit lab they were currently in, one of the researchers found a hidden corridor. They followed it, deep into another tunnel....

There was a distance formula, a calculation that was needed. The formula was brought into the dark tunnel, in Ivanka's purse. At the end of the tunnel, there was a door. Ivanka had never been in this area of the research facility. The door was not locked. They opened it and entered the next area. It truly was amazing to see the next lab. It was state of the art, with what seemed to be a transport module. At the computer console, Ivanka quickly added her calculations into a system. It prompted the sequence for particle collisions. The instructions on the table showed that each researcher could safely fit into the transport car. They entered after Ivanka entered the formula numbers – which started a clock of twenty minutes. The clock started the countdown… and at the end of the count down, She assumed that the particles would travel the length of the surrounding tube – then collide. The collision would propel the transport car up the nano tubule tracks. Where the tracks ended were a mystery….Tommy and Gina were seated next to each other in the transport car. As the clock ticked down, closer to ten minutes… all the researchers were seated in the car, strapped into the seats… Ivanka ensured that the entrance door to the car was closed and locked. They looked forward with excitement. Ivanka believed that the car would quickly propel up the tracks, into the surrounding atmosphere... From what she read in the manual; it was concluded the car was headed for docking in a "space station". When the clock reached five minutes, a recorded computer message was heard in the car... The message emphasized the importance of buckling into each seat. The clock reached one minute... And just like that, with smooth acceleration – almost unnoticeable to the human senses, they arrived. The transport car docked slowly to the station.

They were not in "outer space". Before boarding the next area, the "space station", they discussed where they were. Ivanka hypothesized and referenced a scientific article... In search for other civilizations, outside the planet Earth – it became evident that there were no "viable planets" that were close enough to travel to. Blue-prints were theorized and written to "create" a sustainable platform. The plans were for a planet close enough to Earth, that would have similar physics requirements. Similar, but not the same – since the planet was closer to the "Sun". The planet, Venus, was perfect! Ivanka smiled and chuckled... in a nerdy way. Tommy liked her sense of humor – it was splashed with pure brilliance. Ivanka continued... [she was a young researcher, destined for greatness... anyone that knew her, knew that to be true]. The Earth has sustainability. However, catastrophic events historically have happened and will happen again. There were known risks: a huge asteroid hitting the planet, global warming, resource issues, significant climate change due to many factors (including global warming), pandemics of bacteria, fungi and viral origins....and that were the risks the human population knew about. It was those risks that presented concerns to the future. Even more concerning... were the risk factors that the human population did not know about...because those were the risks that could not be "prepared for". Tommy was young, but he knew that in the research population, that was where the "theories" were presented. The theories of future "risks", the potential problems of the future. Not small problems... no, the problems that had the potential to be a "global killer". So, the result of reading through some of these "theories", was the development of a transport station. And there they were, in the first transport station. The station hovered in the upper atmosphere of Earth. Not completely in outer space, and not completely in the visible atmosphere of Earth. This was the first phase of the research project. After establishing a fully functional "hovering station", in the upper atmosphere of Earth...the next phase was to get over to planet Venus and establish the same type of a full self sustainable station in the upper atmosphere of Venus. The planets surface could not be inhabited. However, it was in the upper atmosphere, where all the critical life sustaining factors were present. Not the same as Earths, but very close, very similar!It was Saturday night. They were not going any further... not to Venus! Gina, Tommy and the researchers were just happy to be where they were.

They would spend the night there. Especially, since they discovered a huge culinary arts section of the station. The area was stocked with food! They also found technical manuals. Ivanka quickly started reading through the literature to gain insight into the possibility of traveling to Venus. Tommy and Gina started cooking a late-night snack. Fascinating stuff! Ivanka yelled out (in her quiet style, which was not really a yell – just a cute whisper...). The hovering space stations were there for one of two reasons. The first was obvious: to offer a new world, just in case there was a catastrophic event on planet Earth. The station in the atmosphere of Venus wa

RICHARD A. BOEHLER, JR.

fully sustainable and there were other areas with stock piles of resources. Ivanka eyes were glowing with excitement. She shined such a bright light of brilliance! It was the second reason that caught the attention of everyone in the room. Almost hard to believe. All the evil in the world, all the evil (soulless) people walking around the planet earth did in fact have a purpose. Sort of a "symbiotic relationship". According to the technical manuals, there was a transfer of "energy" directly to the "Sun". And this was what some would call "HELL". Interestingly, for the Sun to continue to burn, and sustain life as everyone knew it... the continuous transfer of evil (after death) energy to the sun was needed! The professor (Brian) was utilizing the evil energy to bring dead bodies to life, and that stopped Gina. Her face whitened in fear. She knew that she had seen familiar faces of the recent dead, walking around town...

Gina and Tommy finished the late-night snack and shared with all the researchers. Even though they were excited to be in the hovering station, it was late. The researchers were ready to sleep. They found sleeping bags and pillows. There were sleeping quarters. They decided to all sleep in the living room area, together. A nice way to spend a Saturday evening. Tommy snuggled in close with Gina. She liked to sleep on her side. He followed her. Nuzzled in close to the back of her head. Not too close, but close enough to enjoy the vanilla scent of her soft, straight shiny long hair. It was heavenly and quickly placed him into a peaceful sleep. She always insisted in locking her toes and feet into his. Gina and Tommy were asleep, together – with smiles... an indicator of "true love...".

They woke early, the next morning. It was now Sunday. Ivanka took some diligent notes from the technical manuals. She was ready to bring the information back to "University..." to read, learn, extrapolate and apply. The information was relevant to the travel between the Earth space station and the hovering Venus space station. The trip back down to the beach tunnel laboratory was once again smooth and quick. It was a technology that they were not accustomed to. Amazingly efficient and effective – as the car moved along the nano-tracks. Inside the beach tunnel lab – Gina noticed something odd. She remembered that one of the coffins was most definitely empty. Looking through the clear front glass window – she observed a body! The researchers decided to leave as promptly as possible – since they were already into Sunday. They would return for another go at the space travel, though.

The End (continued in chapter 3).

3

Technical Manuals/ Procedures

Living in suburban Long Island towns offered some advantages and disadvantages to youth. The kids were raised in neighborhoods with plenty of space. Some towns were surrounded with vast areas of farm land. Other areas [most of the other areas on long island] were either surrounded by large forest [pine tree forests] or ocean. Tommy and Gina enjoyed visiting the local beaches together. It was always a nice day or a nice weekend to get away and just soak up the sun. There were many different beaches across Long Island. Traveling west from where they lived sometimes offered a concert in the Jones Beach Arena.

Traveling further east of where they lived offered a more silent get away. A time to enjoy a picnic at the very end of Long Island – Montauk Point. Time passed and Gina graduated from High school. Tommy was off for the summer, from University studies. She would be heading out of state for studies at a four-year college down south, in the Virginia area. Tommy would continue studies at University. The projects in the beach tunnel lab continued, year-round. There was much more to investigate. And they would certainly do that. First, thought – Tommy needed to catch a flight. The plane was leaving and he was packed with full military gear. It was a short time that they would be apart. Only two to four weeks – depending on how things went. The night before his flight, Tommy drank way too much beer. Perhaps, there was some hard liquor mixed in with it – that night. He wasn't sure... He was sure that his internal biological systems were completely saturated. Which resulted in "puking". Probably not the best thing to do, the night before taking an airplane! The night air settled and Tommy fell silent, next to Gina. It was always her strawberry blond hair that created a sense of "euphoria". The soft, shiny hair had a way to settle his "heightened wolf-like senses". The scent sealed the process. He was asleep – on his side with her. The night went by to fast – they woke to the alarm at 4 AM. The flight left a local airport at 5 AM. Tommy hugged and kissed and hugged her good bye.

The travel to the airport that early in the morning was always refreshing. Tommy kept the windows open as the cool morning breeze made its way into his car. There was something about coo morning air. The air seemed "cleaner". The air seemed "fresher". The airport was in the distance as the light sun colors breached the sky horizon. There was an area of the airport, that had parking for military. He usually kept his car there – while traveling out of state. The flight left as scheduled with a team of military men and women. They reached the Virginia Naval base in record time. And that was a good thing, since the ship they needed to get to was ready to make sail into the Atlantic-ocean.

They were apart for a few weeks. Closer to a month. In terms of life on Earth.... It was not much time apart at all. Or would be... During that time apart, Gina spent time with the researchers. She was truly a brilliant soul. Ahead of her time... with elegance, humor and kindness. Another weekend approached and the researchers found their way back to the secret beach laboratory. The transport to the upper limits of the atmosphere was on their agenda. Gina brought some magazines this time. She was an avid reader of many different magazines. In fact, she just loved keeping up to date on the fashion trends. Keeping up to date on the newest "conspiracy theories" (a completely different type of magazine, compared to fashion trends!). It seemed so different in the "space station". Gravity for one thing, was very different. Their interest, though, was to figure a way to get out to the next lab. The lab located in the atmosphere of the planet Venus. It was a risky venture. One they were just about ready to embark on. The researchers were top-notch minds in their fields of science. And one aspiring science person, Gina. She had all the right foundational elements for such a venture. There was no doubt about that. And importantly, just the basic zest to move forward...It wasn't the traditional space travel that most people knew about. The premise was built on the nano-transport technology. The elements of such technology were something fierce. Ahead of its time! The strength of a microscopic world. A track that had essentially been built through space and time. The track left the Earth lab and traveled directly to the planet Venus lab. And on the nano-technological track, was a transport car. The car was big enough to transport all of them, together – with plenty of space for magazines, water and snacks!

The travel was smooth, the travel was fast and exciting. Gina and the researchers were essentially dipping into a whole new world! Space travel. And they all agreed that they were not astronauts! That was okay though. They were the adventurous type, the scientist type. Even Gina (being the younger of the researchers, with less experience) was happy to be part of the exploration. Besides that. Gina had new thoughts about government conspiracy theories – especially since she was in route to reaching the space station on planet "Venus"! When the researchers got back to Earth, Gina had planned to get with Tommy. She smiled and thought, it would be official. Tommy would make love to a "space girl"! [Gina chuckled, silently – with a mischievous facial smirk... which she knew Tommy always loved...it was her way of giving him the "bedroom eyes..." an effective way that she had to signal to Tommy that she yearned to share love and affection with him.... That "always" nurtured their souls]. The researchers were amazed at the journey. At the front of the transport car was a panel. The panel clearly showed that their trip would take no significant time at all. Ivanka was wondering if the calculation factored in Einstein's constants for the theory of relativity?

Ivanka finished reading the technical manuals. Gina opened a few snacks and shared with the other researchers. There was good new and bad news. The good news was that this transport capsule was truly ahead of its time! It was completely self-sufficient. It would transport to the Venus atmosphere, where another space station was located. The transport car was buckled onto an extremely strong nano-technology track. The track was at the nano scale, completely invisible to the human eye. The car generated its own oxygen and was powered through the nano tracks. There were emergency protocols. Similar to United States Navy Ships. The great US Navy ships were all (mostly) nuclear powered. The ships could remain out at sea in combat mode for years. No, with replenishment tactics – the ships could remain in war-time readiness (out in various parts of ocean) forever!

And similar to this strategy. That is having a nuclear reactor for a power source in the heart of the ship. So did the space transport car. The nuclear power was only in an emergency though. If there ever happened to be an issue with transport between Earth and Venus, the nuclear protocol would be activated. The planet Venus was actually pretty close to Earth. The distance was incredibly closer than they had imagined. They could already see the planet Venus! The planet was also very similar to planet Earth. With some differences. For one thing. The sun did not rise in the East and set in the West. The planet Venus had a spin that was in a different direction – compared to Earth! The surface was not habitable and even the atmosphere had too much sulfuric acid in it. However, it was in an area of the atmosphere that had a "sustainable condition". That is where the space station hovered... That is where the researchers were heading too.Gina asked "so what's the bad news?". The bad news was that time would change differently with this travel. Looking at the calculations, they would be able to return to Earth, easily. More time would have passed on Earth though. Approximately five years will have passed in their short visit to Venus. Maybe... They were not completely sure... The plan was to board the Venus space station and collect some information.

Find out what in the world was going on with "Dr. Brian's devious experiments". Ivanka suspected that he was harnessing the energy from the sun to bring the "dead to life". Or really, just have the dead become... "the walking dead". The sun was the energy source. The energy transfer of every evil entity on earth went directly to the sun. Or what some would call: "Hell". Gina love the conspiracy theories... She said "sounds good to me! Better than area 51 and little green men!". They all laughed...

And they arrived at the planet Venus. The docking was accurate, and swift. The researchers anxiously left the transport car to an incredibly spacious living station. The station was hovering in the atmosphere of Venus. It was self sufficient with a modern style. Living quarters and areas that they were interested in exploring. However, they did not want to spend too much time in the living station. They would return, when they knew more about what they had stumbled upon. There was a sign for a lab. That was a good place to start. In the near distant hall was a laboratory. Within the quarters were high tech equipment and what looked like "coffins...". Gina realized that these coffins had bodies in each chamber! There were manuals that described the transfer of energy from the sun into this area... Was it possible that this mad scientist – Dr. Brian, found a way to bring this energy into dead bodies? And if that were even possible, did this secret experiment have anything to do with what she had seen around town? Gina talked to the researchers about her sightings of "the walking dead". At first, she thought it was not possible. But, looking at these coffins and seeing the lab equipment... it was becoming clearer that there was something very sinister occurring in this place.

The researchers immediately noticed that the hovering space station was one of many, in the atmosphere of Venus. They were docked on the main hub. Within the corridors of the space station they found a large map that showed twenty space stations, in total that hovered in the atmosphere. Fascinating design, with complete self-sufficiency. The sustainability was made possible with design. The design of each "world", each "city" to just hover within a safe zone of the atmosphere. Above the atmosphere and below the atmosphere were not safe areas. These areas would destroy the living environment with the harsh conditions. There was just too much sulfuric acid and other chemicals. Not to mention, the heat of the planet would instantly melt anything near its surface.

The researchers agreed not to stay more than one night.

Gina was jet lagged from the relatively short journey between Earth and Venus. She asked if it would be okay for her to take a nap in one of the main living quarters. The researchers brought her some pillows and a blanket... While Gina slept, the others sifted through the technical manuals. Gathering information about the situation of this planet, of this "real life living and breathing experiment". Gina dreamed... she felt a part of herself leave...the soul was traveling...this was only possible for people with good souls. And there she was, in another place. A bit intimidating to her. In fact, with a perceived sense of being overwhelmed. Finally, though, she did not feel too much anxiety with her vision. She felt happy, because she was with Tommy.

They were on Earth.

It was the most amazing vision... dream...or reality...was it possible that

Gina, being on another planet [Venus]... could feel Tommy? More than just feel him. They interacted as her soul reached into him. They loved each other in a pool.... They fell asleep together and drove in a car to get an early lunch together... Gina clearly recalled him saying to her that she was a wonderful lover...Tommy went on to make the point that it had nothing to do with her last name. [fame or anything like that had nothing to do with the incredible light that shined from her – not that she was famous, though.] Tommy wanted Gina to know that he would never smother her...He had been through to much [in this life and lives before], he knew the importance of space....it was also good to be together. Together with common goals, at various times. Gina woke from her nap at the Venus space station. The researchers had completed their fact-finding mission. They found food that was easy to prepare.

They were relaxing in the living quarters, when Gina woke from her amazing dream. Ivanka brought some Alanis Morsette alternative music to listen too....to relax too, while they ate and started discussing the findings of this amazing world. Gina liked this music, she always listened to it with Tommy. The music reminded her of Tommy. She missed him. The team of researchers did not stay "off planet Earth" too long. There were just too many unknown variables. Ivanka was concerned about the relativity factor. If they spent the night in the atmosphere of Venus, then returned to Earth the next day.... Would they have aged less than their friends and family on Earth? Would it really be all that significant? They had a good night's sleep. Who wouldn't, rotating around the planet Venus? Wasn't this the planet or "God of Love"? There truly was so much to explore and learn about in the new world... It was an amazing journey for one thing. And the potential for the future was invigorating! The hope for a place to "colonize", to grow, to flourish together. They wondered how long the average human would live, rotating around the planet Venus... Was it a 100 years? Was it 200 years? Perhaps it was longer! As the team traveled back to planet Earth, they discussed their findings in the short visit. There were many formulas and it was some what difficult to sift through. They were good though. Ivanka cut through the technicalities like a "hot knife through butter". Gina laughed and said "Tommy always used that analogy". It was one of the toughest football coaches he trained under. For the coach, it was simple... run down the foot ball field and smash into whoever has the football! Take him down! Cut through everything like a "hot knife through butter", and tackle the son of a bitch!

It was the formulas for "manifest destiny"! Ivanka spoke elegantly – as she always did... conveying the complex information, in a simplified way – an understandable way. Not too much different from the laying of iron tracks across the United States land – in an effort to meet destiny. The destiny called "manifest destiny". Exploration into the unknown territories! And so, there they were – along nano sized railroad tracks – into outer space. The space tracks were the only pragmatic approach. Incredibly strong in structure. And protected within a large clear tube. The tube was polarized – with extremely strong magnets. This was a fail-safe – to repel any outer-space debris that may run into the tubes... There were emergency protocols. Like the self-sufficient nuclear core in each car. The units of the technical formulas were converted to be "like". And looking at the calculations, Ivanka figured that as they returned to Earth... approximately two weeks-time will have passed! The tubes were not connected

RICHARD A. BOEHLER, JR.

at each space station. The connections were open – similar to the synapses at the end of each human nerve. The release of chemical messengers occurred in these special areas – a release of acetylcholine ----which found its' was to the other area. The other area would be "activated" and an action potential would further carry out the reaction (in the human body...). Ivanka was attempting to show that there was a process, in the human body... not to different from the process of space travel! These large tubes were constructed ---- and they just were maintained in orbit, with slight adjustments that were accomplished via "jet propulsion..." It got deep.... They were all happy to be a part of the journey, and they were happy when they came out of the tube to see planet Earth. The car left the space tube and gently floated into and on to another nano track... which silently and efficiently brought them back into the secret underground beach laboratory! They were home, on planet Earth!

In the central area of the laboratory was Tommy. He greeted Gina with a soft, firm hug. Followed with a passionate kiss. The researchers asked Tommy the date? Approximately two weeks had passed, in the overnight stay in the Venus atmosphere! The theory of relativity was true. They were jet lagged from the journey. Tommy with the researchers traveled to the University for some R and R... [rest and relaxation]. The mysterious events of the local Long Island community continued. Gina usually noticed the strange observations during the dead of night. It was something right out of a horror flick. Except, this was not the typical movie. She walked through the town to a local Carvel to pick up some ice cream. It was late, the place was empty – with one last customer for the night... After selecting two soft serve, vanilla ice cream sundaes – she added marshmallow and peanut butter as toppings... with lots of whipped cream. Walking back to her home, where Tommy was – she noticed that dark clouds rolling into the area. Tommy had a long day at University, and fell asleep. She wanted to surprise him with two ice cream sundaes! As she passed the local fire station, from the corner of her eye she noticed a familiar face. He was walking with a slight limp... and a hood was draped over his head. The town was desolate, and she was beginning to think that it would be a good idea to run back to her house. It was only a few suburban blocks from the Carvel. And as the strange hooded body started to make his way toward her... she was startled by the loud sound of a yellow sports car. It was a friend of Tommy's! Rubin stopped and asked her what the hell a pretty lady was doing, all alone at this time of night. Rubin said "get in". She laughed, and went with him. He was a large black football buddy.

She knew him and he was always full of jolly mischief (the innocent type). Gina explained her plan to pick up the ice cream and to surprise Tommy... As he dropped her off, in front of her house – he gave her a high five and a hug. "tell Tommy to keep in touch!".The hooded body that had approached Gina was "the walking dead". The walking dead had started with one body escaping the secret beach lab, when he was thirsty for blood... The army of the dead had grown to five bodies... Gina luckily escaped the encounter that evening. This did not deter the hooded body. He craved blood and his next victim was not too hard to find. The young girl finished her shift, as she cleaned out the last soft serve ice cream machines. After locking the front door, the girl made her way to a darkly lit sidewalk. She had planned to walk home, but would never make it that night. She was abruptly met by the hooded dark entity. He grabbed her with his meaty hooks and violently injected her with a solution of poison. A low dose. Enough to enter her system, where the blood brain barrier could be crossed.

The victim tried to run away, but only stumbled to the ground. The poison was used by the sludge of this local Long Island Community. Very difficult to detect by area hospital emergency rooms. The result of the low dose of poison was subtle but deadly! Her body temperature fluctuated out of a sustainable biological range. This caused serve heart palpations and dizziness... The hooded walking dead grinned as his victim clenched in painful agony. He thought (since he was somewhat intelligent, in the most-evil sense) that the skull was not just one bone. In fact, the skull was made up of many areas of bone – almost 22 different bones. In the adult female, the skull was sutured together – and seemed to be only one bone. But, this was not the case – he knew better. Besides that, the grey matter of the brain was tasty to his palate! These were his thoughts as he rapidly attacked his victim. With the force of a small hammer – he easily removed a few pieces of skull bone and slurped the contents of her brain! Before leaving the scene, the satisfied walking dead took a piece of the skull for his collection. He would add it to the patella bone of his previous victim. The full moon lit the night sky and the breeze of death filled the town – as the hooded man made his way back to the beach laboratory....

The researchers met a few weeks later. They were ready to travel back to Venus. This time, they brought some additional supplies. A video camera, note books, protein bars and water. The trip was pleasant. In fact, the travel was peaceful and exciting to these young group of researchers. They were planning to stay longer, this time. At least one week... maybe two weeks. What they did not know, was that the walking corpse – the evil murderer, sporting the hooded sweatshirt...well, he was again craving blood... he saw the researcher leave the laboratory! The dead corpse now was planning to enter the second transport car, and follow the group to the Planet Venus!

The End (continued in chapter 4).

Venus

The trip up to the Venus space station was pleasant. The researchers lectured Tommy for a good part of the journey. Gina took a nap on his lap, while Tommy listened with curiosity. What an amazing technology! The nano technology was often talked about in physics. He thought it was all just "deep theory", with no real-world applications.During classes at the University, the ability to work the mathematical formula was one thing. And now, Tommy was excited to be in a car – traveling on super strong, invisible car tracks! The nano technology had other real-world applications...and he wondered if they were also being used. For example, the human body has many "organs" with essential life-saving functions. Sometimes, the organ does not work the way it should. The pancreas has a group of cells in it that is responsible for the production of insulin. The insulin moves sugar in and out of cells for storage and use, in the human body [this is routinely happening as the human body needs more sugar – that is glucose – or if the body has too much sugar and the sugar needs to be sent back into a storage cell]. The pancreas has cells that regulate the release of "insulin". Interestingly, and sadly – sometimes the insulin stops being produced. Or, sometimes the insulin gets produced but cannot be process the right way in the human body (there is a desensitization at the receptor sites). Nano technology has theoretically been used to help any human in need of the insulin process. A small, invisible panel [at the nano technology level] can be created that regulates the process of insulin production. The nano panel is surgically inserted into the human body and the regulation of insulin takes place every day (as normally in a healthy human body).

Tommy wondered if the nano tech panels were being used. Why not? He was traveling on an invisible nano tech rail track into outer space!They all arrived at the space station, in the Venus atmosphere. Tommy was amazed at the space in the station (no pun intended). Their plan was to stay at least a week to maybe two weeks. They got situated. Tommy and Gina rushed to a large "sleeping quarters", smiling as they claimed squatter's rights! Ivanka and the other researchers found their sleeping quarters. They spent the night in the living room area of the first space station. Gina brought a Ouija Board and enticed a few of the researchers to join the game! Some of the others explored the areas of the space station. Ivanka came across what seemed to be a "reactor" to transport energy to and from the sun. The energy was not good energy, so to speak…. What this reactor was being used for was not to help grow green plants. The energy transfer was being used as a vector to launch life into dead bodies! It was getting late, as Ivanka continued to read through the technical manuals…. She was starting to get a better understanding of how the energy transport took place and even how it was used to wake the dead. Outer space was silent. The Venus atmosphere was silent and peaceful. Ivanka liked that. She thought she heard the docking of another transport car – at the other end of the space station. Her curiosity for the technical information kept her focus…. [the second transport car docked and the walking dead murderer entered the Venus space station…].

The days passed as the researchers explored the space station. The creature that followed, was lurking in the darkness. He was somewhat intelligent, cunning and pure evil. He waited. He hid. He watched... the researchers enjoyed time on the space station. There were many different things to do. There were plenty of courts to play a game of basketball. There were plenty of electronic gadgets that had a wealth of libraries. In the evenings, they all got together and watched movies in the "living room". Ivanka enjoyed swimming in a nice in-ground pool. Scarlet joined her most days...

It was the last night that they would be "exploring the Venus space station". Even though they really wouldn't mind spending a few more weeks off planet Earth! Scarlet picked a classic scary movie for everyone to watch. A perfect end to the visit! They dimmed the lights in the living room and started the movie. One of the researchers popped plenty of popcorn and was in the process of bringing it into the dark living room when she was stopped by a shady, grotesque figure. It was the walking dead! She screamed! Scarlet quickly turned the lights on. All the researchers jumped to their feet with expressions of fear. Tommy was not there, he must have left to use the restroom?One of the researchers was approached and attacked viciously by this evil creature. He murdered her in cold blood, as the ladies watched in a state of shock. The creature was not hungry, he killed her for sport. There was plenty of flesh to eat... he would quench his thirst for blood soon enough. Right now, he just enjoyed watching the expressions of fear. He enjoyed the smell of blood from his fresh kill! The dark entity made his way toward Gina. He wore a smile on his face as he approached her. She had long, silky blonde hair. The walking dead wondered how her skull would taste...

About an inch from her she was abruptly pushed so hard that she flew a significant distance – across the room. Landing safely near the cushioned couch…Tommy stopped the dark creature. The creature laughed and violently lunged at the legs of his soon to be victim. Tommy took a hard hit to his legs [legs that were not bone, but heavy technologically advanced steel!]– the creature was aggressive. The creature was strong….not strong enough, though. With an expression of curiosity…. With an expression of disbelief, the creature fell to the ground. Tommy stood over the creature, and countered with a quicker attack to the throat. The fangs of Tommy sank deeply into the creature's neck, with precision…. Following this attack, Tommy finished with a violent snap to the neck…the creature lay on the floor, lifeless. Tommy apologized to all the frightened ladies. Gina ran across the room and hugged him – with tears of joy... with tears of fear. Tommy lost his breath. It was his adrenaline.

Tommy asked the researchers if they noticed a port to send this evil creature. A port that was used to send trash into outer space. Ivanka showed him. Together, they removed the creature from the Venus space station.On the trip back to Earth, the researchers took care of their lost Friend [sadly transporting her lifeless body]. Tommy thanked everyone for their bravery. Especially, Ivanka, Gina and Scarlet... They would return to the secret beach lab in a relatively short period of time... They would return, only to be met by the realization that the "walking dead experiment" was deeper than they ever could have imagined...

The End

Printed in the United States
by Baker & Taylor Publisher Services